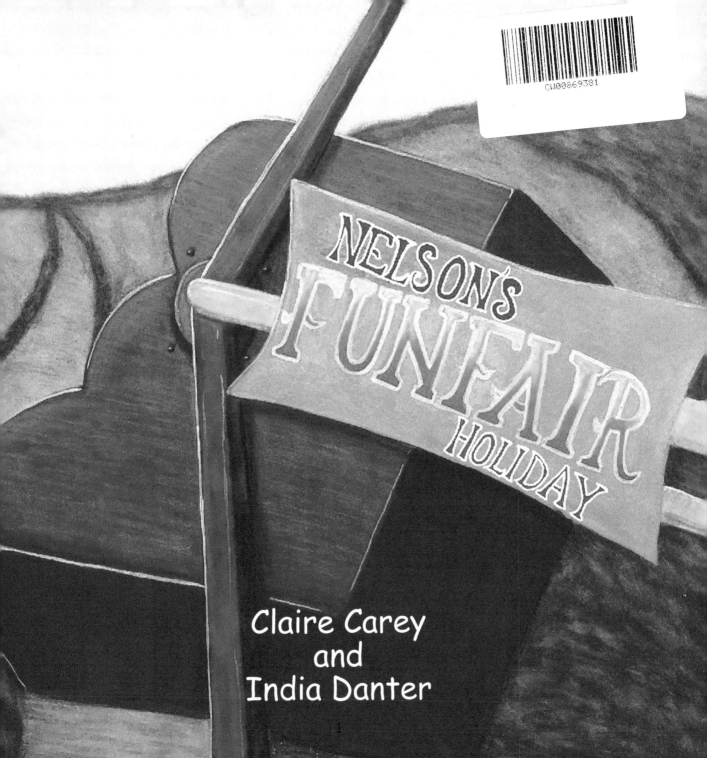

NELSON'S FUNFAIR HOLIDAY

Claire Carey
and
India Danter

illustrated by Inida Danter

First published in the United Kingdom in 2020 by
The Cloister House Press

ISBN 978-1-913460-26-6

Nelson was so excited when he arrived at Auntie Claire's house.

'I'm staying with you at the fair!' he cried.

'Yes, that's right,' said Claire.

Nelson's little face beamed with happiness. Everything was packed ready to leave Gloucester and travel to Ross-on-Wye, to the carnival and fair. Nelson was so excited that he found it difficult to sit still. He didn't realise that it was carnival day as well.

Nelson helped Claire put his bag in the car, and soon he was sitting securely in his car seat with his seatbelt on, ready to go. 'Let's go!' shouted Nelson as the car glided out onto the road.

The journey from Gloucester to Ross-on-Wye is only a short one. Nelson was planning which rides he would go on. 'Auntie Claire,' said Nelson, 'I'm going on the Miami Fever ride.'

'Nelson, you have to be four foot six inches tall to go on that ride, so we will have to check your height first,' replied Auntie Claire.

'OK,' said Nelson, looking disappointed. 'But at least I'll be able to go on all the little rides.' Nelson was quiet for a little while and then asked, 'Will James and Jonathan be at Ross-on-Wye?'

'Of course they will,' replied Claire. 'They can't wait to see you.'

A huge smile lit up Nelson's face. James and Jonathan were Claire's two sons, and Nelson was like a brother to them.

An hour later, Claire and Nelson arrived at Ross-on-Wye, and Nelson was so happy. The fair was just preparing to open.

'Now, Nelson, you must not leave this area,' said Claire as she showed Nelson a map she had drawn especially for him.

'These are your boundaries, and you must stay within them, otherwise I will not be able to see you.'

Nelson understood and linked his little finger with Claire's and promised to stay within the area.

'Good boy,' said Claire, and smiled at Nelson.

Nelson looked around whilst the fair was preparing to open. The fair could not open until all the daily checks had been done, and all the rides had been tested. Nelson gazed around and remembered to stay within the boundaries. He suddenly spotted his friend Cy. With all the excitement, Nelson had forgotten his friend was going to be at the fair. Nelson and Cy were so pleased to see each other and had a long chat about the fair. Nelson remembered that he had to move his bag from the car to the caravan, where he was going to stay for the next few days. The two boys picked up Nelson's bag and placed it in the caravan. Cy's caravan was next to Claire's.

Claire was just making a cup of tea. She asked Cy and Nelson if they would like one, and they both said, 'Yes please.' Both boys sat outside the caravan, chatting and drinking their tea.

6

Cy had his football, so they both went to play until the fair opened. Then Claire called to the boys and took them around the fair, introducing them to every member of staff. Claire told each member of staff that Nelson and Cy were guests, and were allowed to go on the rides and stalls for free, as long as the said 'please' and 'thank you'. Nelson's face lit up.

Claire also showed the staff her boundary map and asked them to inform her straight away if they saw the boys outside the boundaries. The next day was carnival day, and there would be crowds of people everywhere. Both boys listened to these instructions, and Cy said, 'OK, Auntie Claire.'

The fair opened at 2 pm on Friday. Nelson and Cy made their way to the stalls. They remembered what Claire had told them and politely asked, 'Please can we have a go?'

'Yes, of course you can,' was the reply, and Nelson and Cy had lots of fun. Nelson liked the Roll Downs the best, because the prize was a soft toy pug dog.

Nelson really wanted to win that 'Pugo', as he called them. He told Claire that when he was seven years old, he was going to have a dog.

Claire said, 'As long as you look after the dog properly, that will be lovely for you.'

Nelson then quickly replied, 'My dad can do that!'

Claire then replied, 'Your dad has a lot of other things to do, and if the dog is going to be yours, it's up to you to look after it. Pugo will need you to take him for a walk twice a day, and feed him and clean up, especially after he's been to the toilet.'

Nelson looked puzzled. 'I will ask my mum about that.'

Claire shook her head.

'No, Nelson. If Pugo is going to be your dog, you must look after his every need. Mum and Dad are far too busy to take care of the dog as well.'

Nelson was upset by what Claire had told him. Nelson really wanted a dog, but never realised the responsibility it involved. Nelson carried on playing on the Roll Downs until he won a Pugo. Nelson was thrilled, and his face lit up. He thanked the lady when she gave him the prize. 'I'm going to call my prize Pugo. Pugo the dog,' he said, with a big smile on his face.

The next game was Hook-a-Duck. Cy was not interested in this, and went off to play with his football. Nelson's favourite bit was when they threw the duck back into the water tank, and all the water splashed everywhere. After playing Hook-a-Duck, Nelson decided he would like a prize. The member of staff told Nelson that he could have any prize he wanted. Nelson said, 'Thank you.' He was so happy. There were so many prizes to choose from that Nelson did not know which one to have, and spent ages trying to make his mind up. Meanwhile, Cy had returned and Nelson asked him to help him choose a prize.

Cy quickly spotted a Martian dressing-up set, and Nelson decided to take his advice and have that one. He thanked the stallholder and unwrapped the Martian set and put it on. Claire walked over to the boys, and asked Cy where his Martian outfit was. Cy told her that

he had not been playing Hook-a-Duck. Claire said, 'Why don't you have a go, Cy, and if you manage to hook a duck, you could win a Martian outfit as well.'

Within seconds, Cy had hooked a duck and thanked the stallholder for the prize. Both smiling boys were now wearing Martian outfits.

The two boys were having a wonderful time. After all the games, it was time for the rides. They both went over to Nelson's favourite ride, which was Miami Fever. Nelson wanted to go on first, but remembered that Claire had told him you must be four foot six inches to qualify for the ride. Nelson hesitated, as he was unsure how tall he was. With Nelson standing against the height board, the operator of Miami Fever could see that Nelson was not tall enough to ride, but Cy was. 'Sorry, Nelson,' said the operator. Nelson became very tearful and upset, and the operator looked for Claire to explain to Nelson that he was not tall enough.

Claire came over and told Nelson once again, as she had in the car, that you had to be four foot six inches to go on the ride. Nelson cried and said, 'It's not fair. I really wanted to go on that ride and Cy is tall enough and I'm not.'

'That's right,' said Claire. 'Let me double-check. Stand with your back to the height board, and stand up straight this time.' Claire saw that Nelson was tall enough, and told the operator the Nelson could ride on Miami Fever. Claire noticed that Nelson had a big smile on his face as he ran out to his seat. Claire stood thinking, and then she realised what Nelson had done. By now, Nelson was seated on the ride and ready to go. 'Come back here, young man!' shouted Claire.

Nelson could tell by her tone of voice that Auntie Claire was not pleased. He knew what he had done, and he was not going to get away with it.

'Now, stand by the height board again, young man.' This time she placed her hand on top of Nelson's head, and just as she had thought, he had been standing on his tiptoes.

'That was very naughty, Nelson,' said Claire.

'But Auntie Claire, I really wanted to go on Miami Fever. It's my favourite ride.'

'Yes I know all that, and when you are tall enough you can, but not until then. Rules are rules and have to be obeyed. If you are too small, you could fall out. Then what am I going to tell your mum and dad if there is an accident and you get hurt? They would be very upset and angry with me, as I am responsible for you,' said Claire.

Nelson realised what he had done and apologised to Claire. Nelson watched Cy on the ride, and saw that he was really scared, as the Miami Fever goes really fast. Nelson was secretly glad he had not gone on the ride after all.

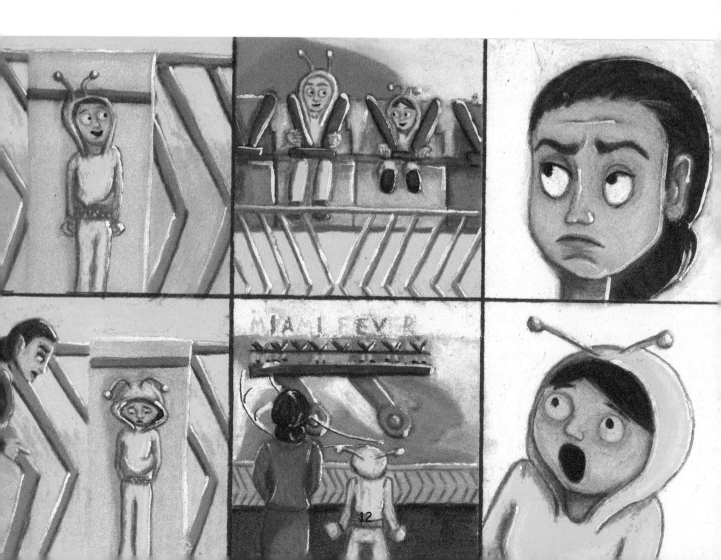

Nelson and Cy made their way over to the next ride, which was the Super Trooper. There was no height restriction on this one, so Nelson was very happy that he was able to enjoy it, sitting next to Cy in the same car. Nelson was not quite sure how high the Super Trooper went, so he was a bit nervous. Before the ride started, Claire walked over to the boys, and noticed how nervous Nelson was. Claire asked Nelson if he was alright and he quickly replied, 'Yes, Auntie Claire. I'm fine.'

'Are you sure, Nelson?' asked Claire again.

Nelson hesitated. 'Auntie Claire, how high will the Super Trooper go?'

'Well, Nelson,' said Auntie Claire, 'see the main pole up there? This ride will lift you to the top of the pole, then tilt in one direction, and then in the other direction. Are you sure you still want to go on this ride?' Claire had noticed that Nelson was still nervous, but he assured her that he still wanted to go on the ride. She also asked Cy if he was OK.

'Yes, I'm fine, Auntie Claire. I've been on Super Trooper before.'

'Perfect.' Claire turned her attention once more to Nelson. 'Would you like me to ride with you, Nelson?' she asked.

'Yes please, Auntie Claire.' Nelson began to relax and looked much happier with Claire onboard.

The ride started, and both boys were laughing. Then the ride began to lift upwards. At first Nelson was fine, but when it started to tilt, Nelson began to feel scared and told Claire he was glad she was with him. She told Nelson to hold on tight.

The next stage was a sixty-five-degree tilt. 'Here we go, Auntie Claire. This is the best bit,' said Cy, who was loving the ride and was smiling from ear to ear. 'This is the best!' he added.

Nelson was still looking a bit nervous, but the ride was soon coming to an end, so no worries. When it finally stopped, Nelson had a look of relief on his face, and Claire asked the two boys if it was good.

'Yes!' they both shouted. 'Can we have another go?'

Nelson now looked more confident and told Claire that he would be fine if they had more rides. Claire told both boys to hold on tight if they had more rides.

'Yes, we will,' they both said, and went on the Super Trooper two more times.

The Ferris wheel was next, which is a very old ride (vintage). Nelson and Cy had been on the Ferris wheel many times before. It was not as fast as some of the other rides, but was high, with great views from the top. After asking politely for a ride, the boys climbed into the car and were locked behind the safety bar by the operator. They were told they had to hold tight and sit still at all times. The Ferris wheel began to turn. It goes round in a circle and the highest point is forty-five feet high.

The boys held tight as the car climbed to the top. It was a lovely view across the whole of the fairground, and Nelson could even see the caravans. He could also see the boundaries that Claire had laid out for him. The boys were at the top for some time as the operator loaded the next passengers into the car opposite theirs. This was to balance the ride, so that it would work better. Nelson realised why Claire had set the boundaries, as the Rope Walk, which is where the fairground was, was near the very wide and fast-flowing River Wye. Nelson had not noticed this before. He told Cy that he now understood why Claire had told him to stay within the boundaries that she had set. 'If we fell in, we would float away, and no one would know where we had gone,' said Nelson. Claire would be very upset, and Cy agreed and said his mum and dad would cry. The Ferris wheel started to move slowly round and round.

At the top the view was great, but at the bottom you could see things at your level. After a couple of minutes, the wheel came to a standstill and both boys got off. Claire was waiting for them. Nelson told her about the river they had spotted, and Claire explained why it was so important to stay within the boundaries she had set. Claire told Nelson it was time for tea, and invited Cy to join them. 'Yes please,' said Cy, smiling.

The boys went around to the caravan. Claire had prepared a picnic ready for the boys, and had spread a blanket on the ground for them to sit on and enjoy their tea in the open air. It was a sunny day, so just right for a picnic. The boys sat quietly, eating their sandwiches and drinking water. They had sandwiches with ham, cheese and pickle, followed by strawberries, blueberries and jelly.

The boys ate everything, and Cy said his picnic was delicious.

Claire said, 'Well done, you two!'

Nelson thanked Claire and asked if they could go around the fair again, and Claire reminded them to stay within the boundaries.

The boys returned to the fair, but neither of them wanted to go on any more rides just yet, as they felt full after their tea. The boys were still wearing their Martian outfits, and so pretended to be Martians. The boys decided they were going to be helpful. They returned to the caravan and asked Claire if she had a bag and a litter picker. Claire went to the back of the caravan, and sure enough she had what they needed.

The boys went back to the fair, Nelson carrying the litter picker, and Cy carrying the bag. The helpful Martians decided to pick up the litter scattered all over the fair.

A member of staff asked them what they were doing.

'We're being helpful Martians, and we're starting by picking up the litter.'

The member of staff looked very pleased, and the boys continued.

After this, the helpful Martians decided to ask each member of staff if they would like anything to eat or drink.

They took their orders, then delivered them. They purchased the drinks and treats from the candy stall within the fair. The staff were delighted with the helpful Martians and thought they were great. The boys took off their Martian outfits and packed them way.

Cy and Nelson decided to go and play in the Fun House. After asking the staff's permission, the boys rushed in and went up and down the stairs, around the roller, then onto the turntables and the moving floor, in and out of the punchbags, and over the rope bridge. The thing the boys liked best was the fireman's bells at the top of the Fun House. They had great fun. They pretended to be pirates, and the Fun House was their ship. They had to defend it from other pirates, who wanted to capture their ship. They carried on playing until the fair was ready to close.

Claire came over to fetch them, as it was time to return to the caravan. Nelson asked Claire if he had to go to bed straight away, and he was pleased when she said he could stay up for a while. Nelson and Cy returned to the caravans as the fair had closed down, and once all the lights were off, the atmosphere had gone. Nelson felt sad, but Claire came to the rescue. 'Don't worry, Nelson, you can do it all again tomorrow,' she said. Nelson felt very happy to hear that.

After the fair was all closed, Auntie Claire, Uncle James, James Jnr, Jonathan and all of Cy's family decided to go to the pub for something to eat and drink. Nelson asked Claire if he could go to the pub as well. 'Yes,' Claire replied. 'I'm not leaving you here on your own, someone might come and steal you.'

Nelson looked a little puzzled.

Claire said, 'If I leave you alone, Nelson – which I'm not allowed to anyway – someone might think, "He looks like a nice little boy, he can come and live with me."'

Nelson asked, 'What do you mean? They would take me forever?'

'Yes, sometimes they do. That's why I don't let you out of my sight and you have a boundary you must stay within, and never talk to people you don't know.' Nelson looked worried, so Claire said, 'You have nothing to worry about but always remember, if you can see me, I can see you.'

Nelson smiled, held Claire's hand, and off they went to the pub. Nelson was really happy now that both families were all going together to the pub. When they arrived, there was a big garden to sit in, as it was still daylight, and nice and warm. Both families enjoyed themselves, talking, eating, drinking and laughing. It was great, just like a party. Nelson asked Claire if he could stay up all night. 'No, Nelson, your mum would be very cross with me if I let you stay up all night.'

'But Auntie Claire, I'm having so much fun.'

20

'I know. This is what you call a special treat, so enjoy it while you can.'

Just after dark, both families returned to the fun fair, wished each other a good night, and returned to their caravans.

Claire had made all the beds before they went to the pub, so the caravan was ready for bedtime. Nelson had a wash in the very little washroom, with the very little sink. But I'm a very little boy, so it suits me, thought Nelson. He put his pyjamas on ready for bed, and climbed in. 'Phew! I'm hot, Auntie Claire,' said Nelson.

Claire said she would open the big vent to allow some air in.

Nelson wondered what she meant, but then watched her climb onto the bed, reach up to the caravan roof and open a really big vent.

'Wow,' said Nelson, looking up at the sky. Claire turned all the lights off, and locked all the doors with a special key.

Nelson looked up at the clear sky, and saw the moon shining, and the stars twinkling in the darkness. 'It's a clear night, so I'll leave the vent open, and you won't get too hot. Good night, Nelson.'

Nelson said good night, and snuggled down into his comfortable bed. He really enjoyed lying in bed, looking up into the night sky, with the silvery moon and bright stars.

If I had a rocket, I could fly around the stars and moon like a Martian, thought Nelson. He drifted off to sleep, thinking how much he really liked the helpful Martians.

Nelson was sleeping, but he could hear noises, so he got out of bed and looked around. Everyone was fast asleep, so Nelson returned to bed. The noise continued, so Nelson once again got out of bed and tried to open the caravan door. To his surprise, the door opened. Nelson quietly stepped outside. The noise was coming from the fairground. Although it was still very dark, the noise was getting louder, so Nelson walked towards the funfair. Suddenly the fair lit up, and Nelson looked around in amazement. He could now see who was making all the noise. It was the Martians! As he looked back towards the caravans, he saw Cy walking towards the fun fair, looking shocked. It was the Martians who had turned on the power and lit up the fun fair. Nelson and Cy were really worried, but when they went back to the caravan, everyone was sleeping soundly.

'What are we going to do?' Nelson asked Cy.

Cy thought the best idea was to ask them to leave, and Nelson agreed.

By now the Martians had managed to open all the stalls and get the Ferris wheel turning.

'Stop! Stop!' shouted Nelson. 'Please leave the fair immediately. It's closed!'

The Martians looked at Nelson and Cy and just laughed, because they were having so much fun. Nelson and Cy looked around in dismay. The Martians were everywhere. They were in the stalls, riding the teacups, going up and down in the jets, and the Ferris wheel was going very fast. The Super Trooper went up and down like a rocket, and they were running around the Fun House, jumping in and out, up and down. The Martians had hooked all the ducks and scattered them around the fair. There was utter chaos everywhere.

Nelson was very distressed and once again asked the Martians to stop, but once again they ignored him. Cy was trying to pick everything up, but as fast as he was picking things up, the Martians were throwing things back out.

This is such a mess, thought Cy.

The Martians were very disruptive and the boys were becoming very tired with their efforts to stop them. The Martians used a special hand signal which seemed to make them laugh, but the boys could not understand them.

'Auntie Claire will be so upset about this,' said Nelson. 'This is my Auntie Claire's fair, and you have made such a terrible mess. I don't know what we're going to do.'

To his surprise, all the Martians suddenly stopped. The Ferris wheel stopped turning, the Super Trooper lowered, and even the Miami Fever came to a halt. The Martians started to tidy up. They were picking up all the prizes and putting the ducks back into the tank. Nelson and Cy were so happy. The Martians were now being so helpful. They even closed the stalls, and once the litter was picked up, they switched off the power and once more the fair was in darkness.

Before they finally left, one of the Martians walked over to Nelson and said, 'Sorry if we have upset you. Please apologise to Auntie Claire.'

Nelson and Cy heaved a sigh of relief. The panic was over. The Martians had gone. There was no trace that they had ever been there. The boys returned to their caravans and went back to bed.

The next morning, Claire woke Nelson up with a nice cup of tea, and Nelson thanked her. 'Did you sleep well?' asked Claire.

Nelson thought for a moment. 'Yes, I did sleep well, but I was woken up by all the noise outside.'

'What noise?' asked Claire, looking puzzled.

'It was those naughty Martians,' said Nelson. 'They were everywhere, and Cy and I had to ask them to leave the fair.'

Claire still looked puzzled, and asked Nelson where the Martians were.

Nelson replied, 'They were everywhere! On the stalls, on all the rides, just everywhere. We couldn't stop them. Sometimes they even used secret hand signals to communicate. When I told them it was Auntie Claire's fun fair, they quickly picked everything up, stopped all the rides and left. Cy also helped to pick the rest of the stuff up.' Auntie Claire looked concerned and checked to make sure the caravan door was still locked.

'I think you were dreaming, Nelson,' said Claire.

'No, Auntie Claire,' said Nelson. 'The Martians were everywhere!'

'I'm sure they were,' smiled Claire. 'Would you like another piece of toast?'

'Yes please,' said Nelson, 'and can I have some jam on it please?'

After breakfast, Nelson had a wash in the little bathroom with the little sink. He liked this bathroom, as it was just the right size for him.

He then got dressed and asked if he could go out.

'Yes,' said Claire, 'but don't forget to keep within the boundaries like I told you. It's carnival day so there will be crowds of people, and it will be a very busy day for the fair. It opens at twelve o'clock.'

Nelson went around to Cy's caravan, to see if he was awake yet. After Nelson knocked, Cy's mum opened the door.

'Cy is still fast asleep,' said his mum.

'OK. I'll call back later,' said Nelson.

Nelson wandered around the fun fair. Uncle James was very busy, making sure everything was ready for the busy day ahead. James Jnr and Jonathan were doing their daily checks, and members of staff were cleaning all the rides. 'Come on, Nelson,' said Jonathan. 'You can help as well.'

Nelson looked a little shocked. 'I'm too little,' he said.

'Well, I can find a little job to suit you,' said Jonathan.

Nelson had a big smile on his face. 'OK, what can I do?'

Jonathan handed him a sweeping brush. 'You can sweep out the Fun House. Start at the top, and work your way down.'

Nelson was very happy to help. He enjoyed sweeping. While he was sweeping, he thought of all the fun he and Cy had had yesterday in the Fun House. Nelson swept it out as he had been told, and saw Jonathan walking towards him. Jonathan looked around and said, 'You've done a good job there. Well done, Nelson.'

Nelson asked if there were any other jobs he could do.

'Yes,' said Jonathan. 'You can make sure the Hook-a-Duck stall has enough prizes for today.' Jonathan opened the stall and showed Nelson where the prizes were kept. Nelson looked around and noticed all the Martian sets had gone. He walked over to where the prizes were kept and filled up the boxes, so there was plenty there for the day. He also filled up the soft toys and dolls, for the busy day ahead.

When he finished on the stall, James Jnr strolled over and said, 'You've done a good job there, well done!' Nelson asked him if there were any more jobs for him. 'Yes, there's one more little job for you,' said James Jnr. The ice cream van had just arrived, and he gave Nelson the money to buy them all an ice cream.

Nelson had a big smile on his face. 'Thank you,' he said excitedly. Nelson bought them all an ice cream, and now everyone else also had a smile on their face. James Jnr said, 'You're a good little worker, Nelson. Well done and thank you for your help.'

Nelson returned to the caravans, and as he drew near, he could see Cy outside, enjoying a cup of tea. Cy's mum asked Nelson if he would like a cup of tea, and Nelson said, 'Yes please.' Both boys sat chatting whilst drinking their tea. Nelson told Cy that the Martians were very naughty the previous night. 'We both needed to stop them from wrecking the place, and throwing things everywhere. You were picking up the prizes and ducks, remember?'

Cy started to laugh and said, 'You were dreaming, Nelson. We didn't go anywhere last night.'

Nelson looked confused. 'Maybe I was, but it all seemed so real.' Nelson asked Cy if he was coming out to play, but Cy had to help his mum before the fair opened, and after that he could go out.

Today was carnival day and Nelson was really excited. He could hardly wait to see the carnival floats. He returned to the caravan and Claire asked him what he had been up to.

'I've been helping James and Jonathan. The Fun House is lovely and clean and the stalls are full of prizes. Best of all, we all had ice creams.'

'Wow!' said Claire. 'You have been a busy and helpful boy. Well done, Nelson. Now let's go and see if my fair is ready for opening.'

After Claire had locked the caravan door, they both made their way to the fair. Claire had a big bag with pockets in, containing money for each member of staff. Claire organised each member of staff, and told them which stall or ride they would be managing. She then gave each person a money pocket. When everything was ready to open, Nelson asked Claire what she would like him to do. Claire told Nelson that he would be helping her but reassured him that he would still be able to see the carnival floats. 'When they arrive, you and I will watch them together.'

Nelson was very happy. 'What will we be looking after today, Auntie Claire?' Nelson was thrilled when Claire told them they will be managing the Dodgems. 'Will I be able to operate it?' asked Nelson.

'No,' said Claire. 'You're not old enough yet.'

'What will I be doing then, Auntie Claire?'

'You can take the money from each customer,' said Claire. Nelson looked a little shocked, and said he was too little to do that job. Claire said, 'Can you count to ten?'

Nelson replied, laughing, 'Of course I can count to ten.'

Claire replied, 'In that case, you can take the money while I operate the ride.'

Nelson was still unsure about taking the money, and asked Auntie Claire how much each ride cost. Claire replied, '£2 per person.'

Nelson stood thinking about this. 'So if there were three people, that would be £6, and if they give my £10, I will give them £4 change?'

Claire was very happy with Nelson's answer. 'There you are. I told you you could do it. If ever you're not sure, I'm here and you can always ask me.'

Nelson was very happy to be helping Claire, and he couldn't wait for the first customer to arrive. 'Auntie Claire, so you don't think I'm too little, then?'

Claire said he was not too little, as long as he didn't let anyone ride for free. Claire told Nelson to stay in the control box with her, so she knew where he was, and wouldn't have to worry about him once the people arrived. Nelson had a good view from the control box and could see Cy helping his dad. Uncle James, James Jnr and Jonathan were also busy, making sure everything was in order.

Finally the first customer arrived. Nelson was waiting patiently, with a big smile on his face. Nelson looked up to the man, and after saying hello, he asked him if he would like a ride on the Dodgems. The man replied, 'Hello, young man. Can I have two please?' He handed Nelson a £5 note, and Nelson quickly gave him £1 change.

Claire was watching. 'Well done, Nelson,' she said.

Nelson was really pleased with himself and couldn't wait for the next customer. Next, a group of teenagers bought tickets, and they had the correct amount of £2 each. The ride was soon almost full, and Claire was busy making sure the ride was ready to start. Nelson sold two more tickets, and the lady handed him a £20 note. He quickly worked out the correct change and remembered what Claire had told him about counting in tens. He handed the lady £16 change. Claire was very pleased when Nelson told her. 'You're a star,' she said, and Nelson felt very happy.

It became very busy and Nelson chatted to the customers, and continued taking money. The girls kept telling him how cute he was, and were laughing and joking with him. The afternoon proved to be a great success, and Nelson enjoyed every minute of it.

After the busy time, the fair went quieter. Uncle James came into the control box and asked Nelson how he was getting on.

'I've taken loads of money, Uncle James!'

'Well done,' said Uncle James.

The floats started appearing and Uncle James told Nelson he could go and watch them. He had been so busy he had forgotten all about them. After asking Uncle James if he would be OK, and he

had told Nelson he would be fine, Nelson went off with Claire. She suggested Cy might like to join them. Nelson shouted in a loud voice, 'Cy, Cy! Would you like to come and see the floats with us?'

Cy asked his mum and she said, 'Yes that's fine, but make sure you stay with Auntie Claire.' Claire told the boys they must stay together, as there were crowds of people there. The floats were all nicely decorated and looked amazing. Nelson spotted a fire engine and shouted to Cy and Claire to go and look at it.

They were allowed to climb on it and inspect it, and chat to the firemen and women. The firemen chatted to the boys and showed them how everything worked, and where the equipment was stored. They were also allowed to sit in the driver's seat. As they walked away from the fire engine, Claire could hear Nelson and Cy saying how they would love to be firemen and drive the fire engine. Then they all went to look around the stalls, before returning to the fun fair.

Nelson and Cy had not seen each other all day, as they had both been busy helping with the fair. Now they both thought it was time to put their Martian suits on and be helpful Martians again. They began by picking up litter. There were large amounts everywhere, and the helpful Martians did a very good job. They also went around asking each member of staff if they needed anything. Some wanted drinks, but even those who didn't want anything thanked the boys for being so kind. Nelson and Cy enjoyed being helpful as it made them feel good to help others. When they were satisfied that no one needed anything else, the boys packed away their Martian outfits.

Nelson asked Cy if he would like to go on the Ferris wheel. Cy said, 'Lets go!' and both boys made their way across the fairground. Cy said the view would be great from the top, as they would be able to see the fire engine and all the floats. After asking the attendant if they could have a ride, both boys were soon fastened into their seats, with the safety bar across. The ride started. They were off! When they reached the top, Cy said, 'What a view!' Nelson pointed out the fire engine, and also the fact that some of the stalls were starting to pack up. Even though there were still plenty of people around, some of them were beginning to drift off home. When they reached the ground, Cy said he had to go and help him mum pack everything away. 'See you tomorrow,' Cy told Nelson.

Nelson decided to go back to the Dodgems control box to see Claire. 'Nelson, I'm glad you're back,' said Claire. 'The fair will be closing soon, so I prefer you to stay here with me now.' Nelson stayed with Claire and they both returned to the caravan together.

Nelson noticed that all the staff were getting changed into their work clothes. 'Will you be taking the fair down tonight?' asked Nelson. Claire said they had to get everything packed away ready to leave. Nelson could see that Cy was helping his mum pack all the soft toys away into large bags, so he offered to help Claire. Nelson wanted to help with the packing, but Claire said he needed to get back to the caravan, so he would not be in the way. Claire was not sure about Nelson helping, as she was worried that he might get hurt. Nelson sighed and followed Claire back to the caravan. Once they were back in the caravan, Claire pulled the curtains wide open, so Nelson could see all the activities. She made Nelson a cup of tea and a sandwich, and he sat watching James Jnr and Jonathan helping Uncle James. They were all working very hard to get everything packed away.

Nelson really wanted to help with the packing and asked Claire once again if he could go out and help. 'Let me finish my jobs, and we will both go out and help,' said Claire. Nelson sat staring out the window. The fairground was gradually disappearing. He noticed that the Hook-a-Duck stall was gone, and all Cy's stalls had been packed away.

Claire suddenly said, 'Look what I've found, Nelson.' She pulled a little pair of overalls out of a cupboard, and a high-visibility vest.

'Is that for me?' asked Nelson excitedly, and Claire helped him put them on. The overalls and high-visibility vest made Nelson look really ready for work.

Claire also put on her high-visibility vest and off they went. Nelson walked over to what remained of the fun fair. Uncle James, James Jnr and Jonathan stopped what they were doing, and turned to look at Nelson. 'Hello,' said Uncle James, 'have you come to help?' Nelson replied that he had, and Uncle James said he had a little job Nelson could do. Nelson looked up with a smile on his face. Uncle James showed Nelson all the little pieces of wood that needed to be picked up, and Nelson set to work straight away. He asked Claire what they were used for, and she told him that the wood helped to support the ride, to ensure the rides were level. Claire helped Nelson pick up all the wood.

When they had picked up all the wood, Claire asked Nelson if he was tired. 'No,' said Nelson, 'I'm fine.'

'OK, Nelson, you can pack the little cables away.' Nelson was a little puzzled and asked Claire to show him what to do. Claire first made sure that all the cables were unplugged from the power supply, and told Nelson to watch her. Claire took the end of the cable, and rolled it into a circle on the ground. She went on pulling the cable, winding it around until she reached the end of it. She then picked up the cable and packed it away. Nelson asked if he could do the next one. Claire watched him while he picked up the cable and wound it into a circle, just as Claire had shown him. 'Well done, Nelson,' said Claire. 'I will pack that one away while you start on the next one.'

After they had packed all the cables away, Claire said that was all they could do. Nelson looked at his dirty hands. 'I think I need to have a shower now,' he said. Claire said he could go into the little bathroom and enjoy a shower.

Claire and Nelson returned to the caravan. Nelson had a shower in the little bathroom, which he liked because it was just the right size for him. Claire had made his bed, so Nelson put on his pyjamas and got straight in. He told Claire that he was very tired. Just then, Uncle James, James Jnr and Jonathan came into the caravan. They had managed to get everything packed away, but they were very hungry. Claire asked if they would all like pizza. They all wanted one so Claire bought pizza for everyone.

Nelson by now had got out of bed. 'I thought you were very tired,' said Claire.

'No, Auntie Claire,' said Nelson. 'I love pizza, so I decided I'm not tired now.'

'OK,' said Claire, 'but after your pizza you must go straight back to bed.'

Nelson loved sitting with Uncle James, James Jnr and Jonathan. They were talking about packing the fair away, and Nelson told them how dirty his hands had been after all the work they had done. Uncle James told Nelson what a big help he had been, and Nelson gave a great smile. 'I like working, Uncle James,' he said. Claire came back with pizza for everyone, including Cy and his family. They all sat enjoying it. 'That was the best pizza that I've ever had,' said Nelson.

After everyone had finished, Claire told Nelson to wash his hands and reminded him that it was time for bed. By now, Nelson was really tired. 'I've had a great day, Auntie Claire, thank you!'

The next day, the funfair had to be moved to the next place. When Nelson woke up, Uncle James, James Jnr and Jonathan were already up and out. Nelson asked Claire where the fair was moving to next. She told him they were going to Eastnor Castle, near Ledbury.

'Wow!' said Nelson. 'Will the Queen be there?'

'No,' replied Claire, 'but there may be soldiers at the castle.' Claire told Nelson that many years ago, there may have been soldiers there, and the Queen may have been there at some point, but not now.

'Will I be able to go inside the castle?' asked Nelson. Claire said maybe, but she was not sure.

Uncle James appeared. 'Will you get the caravan ready to leave?' he asked.

'Give us twenty minutes and we'll be ready, won't we, Nelson?' replied Claire.

Nelson jumped out of bed, and Claire told him to brush his teeth and have a wash. Meanwhile, Claire packed the beds away, wrapped the television up, and made sure everything was ready for the road. When Nelson was ready, Claire said they had to go outside and make sure the caravan was ready for travel. She put the jacks up on the caravan and hitched it up to the jeep. They were ready to leave Ross-on-Wye. Nelson took a last look around, remembering the good times he and Cy had enjoyed together.

Nelson wandered over to Cy's caravan. He had been helping his mum and was ready to leave. He said goodbye to him, but felt very sad.

'Will Cy be at Eastnor Castle?' he asked. Claire said he would not. Nelson saw the Super Trooper was all packed and ready for the road, and Uncle James was in the lorry, ready for the off. Claire asked if Nelson would like to ride in the lorry.

Nelson replied very quickly, 'Yes please! I would love to ride in the lorry with Uncle James.'

Claire helped Nelson into the lorry, and made sure he was strapped in. 'Make sure you sit still and be good,' she said. 'See you at Eastnor Castle.' With that, they were off, heading for Eastnor Castle and leaving Ross-on-Wye.

On their way to Eastnor, Nelson thought about the good times, and all the fun he had had with Cy at Ross-on-Wye. He felt sad that it was all over and they were leaving.

As Uncle James drove the big lorry through Ross-on-Wye, everyone stopped what they were doing and came out to watch the fun fair leaving. Nelson loved this, and waved to everybody who looked at the lorry, and they waved back. Nelson could see everything from the lorry as it was so much higher than being in a car.

Having left Ross-on-Wye, Uncle James made his way to Eastnor Castle. Nelson had a great view from the lorry, and he could see sheep and cows grazing in the fields. He could see the rolling hills, and beautiful scenery around the countryside. Uncle James asked Nelson if he felt OK. Nelson told him how sad he felt leaving Ross-on-Wye, but he was looking forward to Eastnor Castle.

'Not long now,' smiled Uncle James.

It was quite a short distance between Ross and Eastnor Castle. As they approached the castle, Nelson could see the towers and battlements. It looked very nice, but smaller than Nelson had expected. Nelson had seen bigger castles before, but they had been in ruins. Eastnor was intact and Nelson asked Uncle James if he would be allowed inside. 'I'm not sure,' said Uncle James. 'We will have to ask if the castle is open to the public.'

They arrived at Eastnor Castle, and Claire pulled up alongside them, towing the caravan. Claire walked up to the lorry and helped Nelson out of the cab. 'Well, we made it,' said Claire, smiling.

Nelson and Auntie Claire's fair arrived safely in Eastnor. Nelson looked around as, one by one, Claire's lorries arrived with all the rides. Straight away, Uncle James assembled them in the correct places. As he looked around, Nelson could see many large tents, rather like circus tents. Claire and Nelson walked over to one of them and walked inside. It was massive. Nelson asked what all the tents were for. Claire said, 'Much more fun, Nelson. This is a fantastic festival called Lakefest.'

Nelson was pleased and asked Claire if he could stay with her for a few more days. 'We'll have to ask your mum and dad,' she said, and Nelson smiled hopefully.

First I would like to say thank you to India Danter for the excellent illustrations.

Next I need to thank my nephew for spending time with us whist on our travels and reminding me just how much fun it was growing up on a fairground.

Also a big thank you to Mrs Cherry Jones for your support and guidance on writing this my first book.